SKYLARK CHOOSE YOUR OWN ADVENTURE® • 49

"I DON'T LIKE CHOOSE YOUR OWN AD-VENTURE® BOOKS. I *LOVE* THEM!" says Jessica Gordon, age ten. And now, kids between the ages of six and nine can choose their own adventures too. Here's what kids have to say about the Skylark Choose Your Own Adventure® books.

"These are my favorite books because you can pick whatever choice you want—and the story is all about you."
                                                        —**Katy Alson,** *age 8*

"I love finding out how my story will end."
                                                        —**Josh Williams,** *age 9*

"I like all the illustrations!"
                                                        —**Savitri Brightfield,** *age 7*

"A six-year-old friend and I have lots of fun making the decisions together."
                                                        —**Peggy Marcus,** *(adult)*

Bantam Skylark Books in the Choose Your Own Adventure® Series
Ask your bookseller for the books you have missed

RACE OF THE YEAR

R.A. MONTGOMERY

ILLUSTRATED BY SUSAN TANG

A BANTAM SKYLARK BOOK®

NEW YORK • TORONTO • LONDON • SYDNEY • AUCKLAND

RL 2, 007–009

RACE OF THE YEAR

A Bantam Skylark Book / May 1989

CHOOSE YOUR OWN ADVENTURE® is a registered trademark of Bantam Books, a division of Bantam Doubleday Dell Publishing Group, Inc. Registered in U.S. Patent and Trademark Office and elsewhere.

Original conception of Edward Packard
Skylark Books is a registered trademark of Bantam Books, a division of Bantam Doubleday Dell Publishing Group, Inc. Registered in U.S. Patent and Trademark Office and elsewhere.

Cover art by Susan Tang
Interior illustrations by Susan Tang

ISBN 0-553-15696-9

Published simultaneously in the United States and Canada

Bantam Books are published by Bantam Books, a division of Bantam Doubleday Dell Publishing Group, Inc. Its trademark, consisting of the words "Bantam Books" and the portrayal of a rooster, is Registered in U.S. Patent and Trademark Office and in other countries. Marca Registrada. Bantam Books, 666 Fifth Avenue, New York, New York 10103

PRINTED IN THE UNITED STATES OF AMERICA

CW   0 9 8 7 6 5 4 3 2 1

RACE OF
THE YEAR

READ THIS FIRST!!!

Most books are about other people.

This book is about you, and what happens to you and your uncle Bill's racehorse, Straight Shooter.

Do not read this book from the first page through to the last page. Instead, start at page one and read until you come to your first choice. Decide what you want to do. Then turn to the page shown and see what happens.

When you come to the end of a story, go back and try another choice. Every choice leads to a new adventure.

Are you ready to race Shooter in the Kentucky Derby? Then turn to page one . . . and good luck!

"Just a few more minutes," you say sleepily as you feel your mother nudging you awake. She nudges again, harder this time.

"Okay, I'm up," you say, flinging the covers back.

You sit up and look around. Then you begin to laugh. It isn't your mother. It's your Uncle Bill's horse, Straight Shooter. And you're not home. You're on the floor of a horse stall at Churchill Downs.

With a twinge of excitement, you remember why you're here. Today is the biggest horse race of the year. It's Kentucky Derby day. And Straight Shooter is entered.

"Hungry, aren't you, Shooter?" you ask.

The horse nods his head and stamps his right front hoof impatiently. Not only is Shooter fast, he's smart too.

"We'll see what we can do about that," you say as you quickly roll your sleeping bag up and get ready for morning chores.

Turn to page 2.

2   As you groom Straight Shooter's glossy brown coat, you think about how far the horse has come in just a few short years. Shooter didn't look like much of a racehorse when Uncle Bill first brought him home. He was just a year old and small for his age. Then Shooter started to grow, just like your uncle predicted. Fred Grady, a famous racehorse trainer and an old friend of your uncle's, came out of retirement to train him.

From the first day Shooter arrived, you have been his stable hand. Every day you muck his stall, brush his coat, feed him oats, and watch him train. Right from the start you knew Shooter was a winner. Today is his chance to prove it.

There's only one problem. Some of the other racehorse owners are jealous. Fred Grady has heard a rumor that someone is going to ruin Straight Shooter's chances. You know there are many ways to hurt a horse or just keep him from running well. Every night since, you've stayed right in Shooter's stall to keep watch.

Turn to page 9.

"Time to pick our starting position," Uncle Bill says and smiles.

"Whatever you do, don't take your eyes off Shooter," Fred warns. "We've made it this far. We have only a few more hours to go."

"Don't worry about that," you answer. Shooter snorts and waves his head, as if he agrees with you.

The two of them leave. You use the free time to polish your riding boots. Shooter quietly munches some hay. Fifteen minutes pass. Then twenty. When a half hour has gone by, there's a sudden sharp knock at the door of the stall.

A tall man enters. He's wearing a suit. "Are you related to Bill Kirkpatrick?"

"He's my uncle," you answer.

"He's had an accident in the parking lot. He was hit by a car. Fred Grady wants you to go in the ambulance. He'll come back to stay with the horse," the man announces.

Turn to page 46.

6   You decide for better or worse to go help Uncle Bill. If he's seriously hurt, he may really need you. The man gives you directions to the accident and promises to stay with Shooter until Fred arrives.

Churchill Downs is crowding up for the race. You try to run, but you can barely squeeze through the swarms of people and horses moving about. When you reach the parking lot, you spot a crowd of people huddled near an ambulance.

"Uncle Bill!" you yell, sprinting the last hundred feet.

Turn to page 10.

"How's our friend doing today?" Uncle Bill
asks, poking his head over the stall.

"Great," you reply, as you finish laying down fresh bedding.

Shooter looks up from his oats and whinnies hello. Moments later he whinnies again when Fred Grady appears.

"Everything okay last night?" Fred asks.

"Yup. Not a thing out of the ordinary," you reply.

Fred begins to ask you a question about Shooter's appetite when he is interrupted by the loudspeaker system. "All owners and trainers report to Racing Committee headquarters in five minutes. Attention. All owners and trainers to Racing Committee headquarters in five minutes."

Turn to page 5.

10   Several people look up as you burst forward.

"Are you related to this woman?" an ambulance attendant asks, gesturing toward an elderly woman being loaded onto a stretcher.

"Woman? What woman? It's my Uncle Bill. He was hit by a car!" you cry.

"I'm afraid you've got the wrong person," someone says. "This woman was hit by a car. We don't know her name, and we can't find her friends."

You stop dead in your tracks. A funny, icy feeling shoots up your spine. You've been tricked into leaving Shooter alone! What if something happened to him? Uncle Bill will be furious!

You are about to tear back to the stall when you notice a booth at the edge of the parking lot marked Churchill Downs Security.

If you decide to run to the security office and get help, turn to page 19.

If you decide to run back to Shooter's stall, turn to page 31.

"I'm sorry, but I have orders to stay with **13**
Shooter. I can't leave. And I'm sure my uncle
would agree with me," you tell the man, "if he
could," you add in a quieter voice.

The man turns red in the face and begins to
laugh. "I was just kidding. Your uncle hasn't
been hurt. He's a great friend of mine. He's always bragging that you won't let Straight
Shooter out of your sight. I just wanted to
check for myself. Say hello for me when he
returns," the man laughs, tapping you on the
shoulder with a rolled-up program.

"But what's your name?" you ask. The man
doesn't seem to hear you and hurries off.

Turn to page 17.

14   You decide to look at the other horses first and eat later. You walk along the stalls and peer inside. Certain Prince looks overexcited. Jump Up is foaming too much after her workout. Desperate Devil snorts regally as you pass. He's Shooter's biggest competition.

You are on your way to the next block of stalls when a jockey you don't recognize runs up.

"Are you related to Bill Kirkpatrick?" he asks eagerly.

"Yes, he's my uncle," you reply.

"They're looking for you. José Verdi has gotten ill. They need you to ride," he tells you.

"Me? To ride in the Kentucky Derby?" you cry.

Turn to page 20.

16   Time passes quickly. By race time, you have practically forgotten this morning's episode.

Uncle Bill has picked starting position number five in the lottery. That means Shooter will be five places from the inside of the track. It's a perfect position, and Shooter is second favorite to win.

Turn to page 24.

What a weirdo, you think with a shrug. **17**

A few seconds later Uncle Bill and Fred return. They're both excited. Uncle Bill picked a great starting position in the lottery—number five.

"Why don't you have a walk around while there's still time? José is supposed to show up around ten to give Shooter a warm-up," Uncle Bill says. José is Shooter's jockey, and this is his first time riding in the Kentucky Derby.

You've actually wanted to take a look around. There are a million things to see, and the race grounds are already getting crowded.

Then you remember, "Oh, some friend of yours stopped by. He said to say hello, but he didn't leave his name."

Turn to page 22.

You run up to the security booth and bang **19**
wildly on the door.

"Hey, take it easy," a man says, opening it.
"It's only made of wood."

"I'm Bill Kirkpatrick's stable hand," you blurt
out. "He owns Straight Shooter, an entry in the
Derby. Someone may be trying to kidnap him,
or drug him, or worse."

The security man turns to you. "Run that by
us again, a little slower this time."

You go over the incident at the stall and the
rumors Fred Grady heard. You describe how
one of you has been with Shooter around the
clock for the past ten days. "Please try to do
something," you beg. "I know something isn't
right."

"We're just track security. But I'll call in the
official police and notify the exit points to hold
all horse travel until we get this thing straight-
ened out."

"Thank you, thank you, thank you!" you
exclaim.

Turn to page 27.

20   You run back to Shooter's stall. Two members of the Racing Committee are deep in conversation with Fred Grady.

"Have you heard?" your uncle calls as he runs up. "We need you to ride Shooter in the race. José is sick."

"But I've never raced before," you say, looking up nervously at your uncle.

"We know that, but you're a good rider, and Shooter knows you better than anyone else, even José. Fred thinks it's too late to substitute a strange rider. He doesn't think Shooter would like it. Fred feels you're our best shot."

"Okay." You nod, barely realizing what you're about to do.

You quickly head off to dress and register for the race. Although you're only a kid, few of the jockeys are taller than you. Small jockeys mean the horse has less to carry. Sure enough, José's racing silks fit you like a glove. A few jockeys tease you, but you don't have time to notice.

Turn to page 29.

What happens next is like a bad dream. Within seconds of starting, Shooter is at the rear of the pack, and he falls farther and farther behind. By the time a winner crosses the finish line, Shooter is twenty lengths back. Your uncle is puzzled and very disappointed. So is Fred Grady. Shooter ran so well at practice. You wonder what could have gone so wrong.

You tell your uncle the story about the strange man. An identity check is performed on Shooter. Sure enough, the horse José rode in the Derby was not Shooter.

You spend the rest of the week describing the tall man in the suit again and again to the police. An investigation is mounted. But no trace of Straight Shooter or the criminal is ever found.

The End

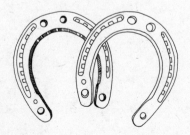

22   "He'll probably stop by later," Uncle Bill says cheerily. "Now you go have a good time," he says, pressing a few dollars in your hand.

You suddenly realize how hungry you are. You want to get something to eat. But you'd also like to check out the other Derby entries and jockeys.

If you decide to go get breakfast,
turn to page 32.

If you decide to look at the other Derby
horses, turn to page 14.

24 The band is playing "My Old Kentucky Home." You proudly walk Shooter to his starting position past the roaring crowds. As soon as the last horse is in the starting gate, the judge fires the starting pistol, and they're off!

Turn to page 21.

Both men get busy on their walkie-talkies calling the exit points to hold horse traffic. In a few minutes the police are notified as well.

"I can't get through to Exit B, Tom," Weatherby says.

"That's odd, Weatherby," Tom replies. "Maybe their machine is off? Let me try."

But Tom has no luck either. He looks at a map of the racetrack grounds. "Hmmm. That exit is right near the stables," Tom says. "It's probably the exit someone would use if they were trying to move a horse quickly."

"Oh, no," you whisper. Then you get an idea. "Is Exit B very far?"

"About two minutes if you run," Weatherby answers. "But the police should be here any second. This could be dangerous. Why don't you let them go?"

If you decide to run to Exit B yourself,
turn to page 35.

If you decide to wait for the police,
turn to page 43.

Fred meets to discuss strategy with you.

"You've got a perfect starting position," he begins. "Shooter will jump out in front. That's his habit. Head immediately for the inside of the track. Ride him at his own speed for the first mile. Start to put the pressure on as you round the last post. Do you understand?"

"I'll do my best," you reply, trying to sound confident.

Turn to page 50.

You turn on your heels and run as fast as you can. When you reach the stall, Uncle Bill and Fred Grady are talking with some reporters. When your uncle spies you, he introduces you to the crowd. Flashbulbs go off, but you ignore them.

"Where's Shooter?" you cry wildly.

"Right there," Uncle Bill points with his cigar. "I told you the kid was crazy for the horse," he adds. The reporters all laugh.

You take another look. It's Shooter all right, happily munching away.

Or is it? Something seems off, but you can't put your finger on it. The reporters stay for several more minutes. Then José, the jockey, arrives to give Shooter a short warm-up run. You sit alongside the track with Fred and Uncle Bill to watch. They don't mention your absence. You decide not to say anything about it either.

Besides, Shooter is running well. If anyone would sense something's off, it would be José. But when he unsaddles, he doesn't mention a word.

Turn to page 16.

32   You go over to the concession stands. Already the lines are very long with people buying coffee and soft drinks.

You wait patiently for your turn. But the line seems to take forever. Finally you place your order and collect your breakfast.

You notice that the clock says 10:05. You have plenty of time before the race. You eat leisurely and walk back to Shooter's stall.

Turn to page 39.

"If I wait for the police, it might be too late," you say. "I've got to get back to Shooter right away!"

"Okay," Tom agrees. "But I want Weatherby to go with you. I'll follow with the police."

You and Weatherby take off at a run. Tom watches from the steps of his booth as the two of you disappear around the corner, heading in the direction of Exit B. It is the last anyone ever hears or sees of both of you.

Your uncle is brokenhearted. But Shooter takes your disappearance even harder. Although by race time he is favored to win, he places dead last.

The End

36 You are so relieved you begin to tremble. Before you know it the police arrive. They begin to ask you questions, and dispatch someone to find your uncle.

Suddenly you hear loud popping noises in the distance. The policemen turn their heads in alarm.

"That's gunfire, and it's coming from the direction of Exit B!" an officer says, quickly drawing his gun.

Turn to page 47.

When you get back to the stall, there's a **39** commotion in full swing.

"What's going on?" you ask, suddenly feeling alarmed.

"It's José," your uncle exclaims, referring to Shooter's jockey. "He's got food poisoning. We had to find a replacement at the last minute. We wanted you to ride, but we couldn't find you in time."

Your heart sinks at your uncle's words. A chance to actually ride in the Kentucky Derby, and you missed it! It's flattering that your uncle even considered you. But it's no consolation for your disappointment.

"We had to take Joachim Concha. He was the only jockey still available. I guess we're lucky the Racing Committee even allowed us a substitute," your uncle says.

There is nothing for you to do now but what you regularly do to prepare Straight Shooter for a race. Somehow, though, your spirits just aren't in your work.

Turn to page 42.

40   Seconds later the man is under arrest. Uncle Bill comes up and exclaims, "What's going on here?"

"This man was trying to make off with your horse, I'm afraid," a policewoman says gently.

"But Shooter is right in his stall," your uncle protests.

"I'm afraid he's not, sir," one of the police says. "That horse you have is probably a dead ringer for your horse, Shooter. But I think that this is the real horse right here."

You open the van door and lead the horse outside. "It's Shooter for sure," you announce.

"But how do you know?" Uncle Bill asks, still having a hard time believing everything.

"Here," you say, pointing to the underside of Shooter's halter. "I put a piece of bubble gum here so I would always have a way to check."

"Smart stable hand you've got there," the chief of police says as he laughs.

The End

42   You regain some enthusiasm as the race approaches. You're sitting in the owner's area with your uncle and Fred. The start of the race begins suddenly, the exact moment that the last entrant is in place behind the gate.

Shooter bursts forward. Only one other horse, Desperate Devil, is ahead.

"Come on, Shooter, go!" you scream. The crowd around you is so loud you can't even hear your voice.

Shooter runs a strong race, and Joachim handles him well. Before you know it, Straight Shooter's name flashes up on the huge screen. He's finished second!

Turn to page 51.

No one would believe you anyway, you **43** think. There's nothing you can do until the police arrive. In the meantime, you just hope nothing happens.

A few minutes later the walkie-talkie buzzes.

"Parking Lot Security, do you read us? Exit B here. I repeat, do you read us?"

"Yes, we just called as a matter of fact. There's a Derby entrant that may have been kidnapped. Hold all horses at checkpoint until notified by the police in person. Do you read?"

"Understood. And don't worry. No horse has left in the past half hour," the box squawks back. "Wait. A horse van is coming now. We'll call if anything looks fishy. Over and out."

Turn to page 36.

The procession to the starting gate moves quickly. People yell your name and shout "Good luck!" from the sidelines. One by one the horses are placed in the narrow starting gate. You watch carefully as the last horse slips into place. A loud bell rings and a voice booms, *"And they're off!"*

Turn to page 48.

46 "Hit by a car! Is he hurt badly?" you cry.

"They're not sure. The ambulance will be here any minute," the man answers.

You are about to do as the man asks when you remember Fred's words. *"Whatever you do, don't take your eyes off Shooter."*

If you decide to go to your uncle Bill, turn to page 6.

If you decide to stay and wait for Fred, turn to page 13.

All of you run toward Exit B. Sure enough, a **47** horse van with four blown tires sits ten yards past Exit B. The driver had obviously broken right through the closed metal gate.

"That's him!" you cry, pointing at the tall man in the suit. "He's the one I left with Shooter."

The tall man is standing alongside the van with both hands on his head while a security agent frisks him. From inside the van you hear a high-pitched whinny. Shooter has recognized your voice!

Turn to page 40.

48 Sure enough, just as Fred predicted, Shooter breaks away. You head toward the inside track. The sound of dozens of hooves pounding earth fills your ears.

"Come on, Shooter," you yell, leaning even tighter into his back.

As if by magic, he puts on an extra burst of speed. The two of you pull away from the pack. By the time you round the last post, you are a full two lengths up. Seconds later, Shooter crosses the finish line in first place.

You are the youngest jockey in the history of horse racing to win the greatest race of them all, the Kentucky Derby!

The End

Straight
Shooter

50   You have less than an hour before the race begins. The press has heard the news, and everyone is dying to get the scoop on the "Child Jockey." Fred and Uncle Bill do their best to keep the reporters and spectators away so you can relax a little.

The time passes quickly. Before you know it, you are weighing in, carrying Straight Shooter's saddle. A stable hand from another stable helps hoist you into it and adjusts the stirrups. You look around at the crowd.

Suddenly you remember a day last month when you were riding Shooter across an open field. You flew like the wind.

"All we have to do today is what we did that day, Shooter," you whisper. The horse whinnies in reply.

Turn to page 45.

Your uncle and Fred Grady are jubilant. Second place is terrific for an unknown horse. Besides, there are other big races this season. And Shooter will be valuable for breeding other racehorses. Within a matter of minutes, your uncle has become a rich man.

But you still feel that if you'd been able to ride, Shooter might have won.

That night at a celebration dinner, your uncle promises you Shooter's first colt as a gift for all your help.

Who knows? In three years' time, you may be back at the Kentucky Derby riding your own horse!

The End

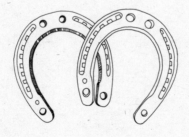

ABOUT THE AUTHOR

R.A. Montgomery is a graduate of Williams College. He also studied in graduate programs at Yale University and New York University. After serving in a variety of administrative capacities at Williston Academy and Columbia University, he cofounded the Waitsfield Summer School in 1965. Following that, Mr. Montgomery helped found a research and development firm specializing in the development of educational programs. He worked for several years as a consultant to the Peace Corps in Washington, D.C., and West Africa. He is now both a writer and a publisher.

ABOUT THE ILLUSTRATOR

Susan Tang was born in Brooklyn, N.Y., and graduated from Pratt Institute. She has been illustrating books for eight years and has done work for Bantam, Scholastic, Pocket Books, Dell, and Knopf. She now lives in Lawrenceville, N.J., with her husband, who is also an illustrator, and their two sons.

CHOOSE YOUR OWN ADVENTURE

SKYLARK EDITIONS

Special Offer
Buy a Bantam Book
for only 50¢.

Now you can order the exciting books you've
been wanting to read straight from Bantam's
latest catalog of hundreds of titles. *And* this
special offer gives you the opportunity to purchase
a Bantam book for only 50¢. Here's how:

By ordering any five books at the regular
price per order, you can also choose any other
single book listed (up to a $5.95 value) for only
50¢. Some restrictions do apply, so for further
details send for Bantam's catalog of titles today.

Just send us your name and address and
we'll send you Bantam Book's SHOP AT
HOME CATALOG!